First published in Great Britain 1996
by Victor Gollancz
An imprint of the Cassell Group
Wellington House, 125 Strand, London WC2R 0BB

Copyright © Angel Dominguez 1996

The right of Angel Dominguez to be identified as author of this
work has been asserted by him in accordance with the Copyright,
Designs and Patents Act, 1988

A catalogue record for this book is
available from the British Library

ISBN 0 575 06339 4

Printed in Hong Kong

The TWELVE DAYS OF CHRISTMAS

Angel Dominguez

VICTOR GOLLANCZ
LONDON

On the first day
of Christmas,
My true love sent to me
A partridge in a pear tree.

On the second day
of Christmas,
My true love sent to me
Two turtle doves, and
A partridge in a pear tree.

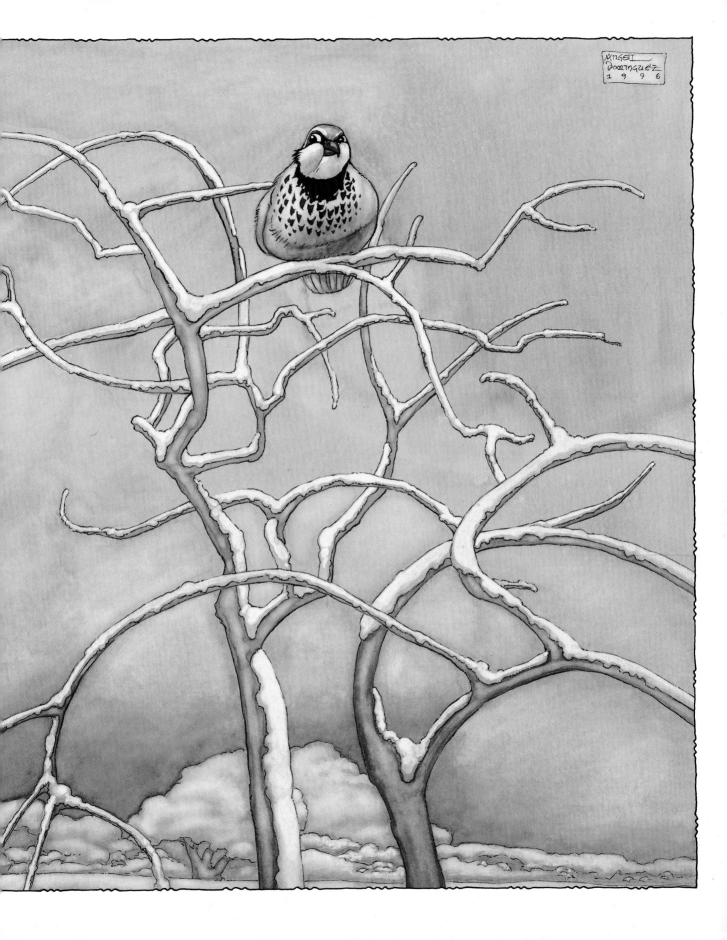

On the third day
of Christmas,
My true love sent to me
Three French hens,
Two turtle doves, and
A partridge in a pear tree.

On the fourth day
of Christmas,
My true love sent to me
Four colly birds,
Three French hens,
Two turtle doves, and
A partridge in a pear tree.

On the fifth day
of Christmas,
My true love sent to me
Five gold rings,
Four colly birds,
Three French hens,
Two turtle doves, and
A partridge in a pear tree.

On the sixth day
of Christmas,
My true love sent to me
Six geese a-laying,
Five gold rings,
Four colly birds,
Three French hens,
Two turtle doves, and
A partridge in a pear tree.

On the seventh day
of Christmas,
My true love sent to me
Seven swans a-swimming,
Six geese a-laying,
Five gold rings,
Four colly birds,
Three French hens,
Two turtle doves, and
A partridge in a pear tree.

On the eighth day
of Christmas,
My true love sent to me
Eight maids a-milking,
Seven swans a-swimming,
Six geese a-laying,
Five gold rings,
Four colly birds,
Three French hens,
Two turtle doves, and
A partridge in a pear tree.

On the ninth day
of Christmas,
My true love sent to me
Nine drummers drumming,
Eight maids a-milking,
Seven swans a-swimming,
Six geese a-laying,
Five gold rings,
Four colly birds,
Three French hens,
Two turtle doves, and
A partridge in a pear tree.

On the tenth day
of Christmas,
My true love sent to me
Ten pipers piping,
Nine drummers drumming,
Eight maids a-milking,
Seven swans a-swimming,
Six geese a-laying,
Five gold rings,
Four colly birds,
Three French hens,
Two turtle doves, and
A partridge in a pear tree.

On the eleventh day
of Christmas,
My true love sent to me
Eleven ladies dancing,
Ten pipers piping,
Nine drummers drumming,
Eight maids a-milking,
Seven swans a-swimming,
Six geese a-laying,
Five gold rings,
Four colly birds,
Three French hens,
Two turtle doves, and
A partridge in a pear tree.

On the twelfth day
of Christmas,
My true love sent to me
Twelve lords a-leaping,
Eleven ladies dancing,
Ten pipers piping,
Nine drummers drumming,
Eight maids a-milking,
Seven swans a-swimming,
Six geese a-laying,
Five gold rings,
Four colly birds,
Three French hens,
Two turtle doves, and
A partridge in a pear tree.